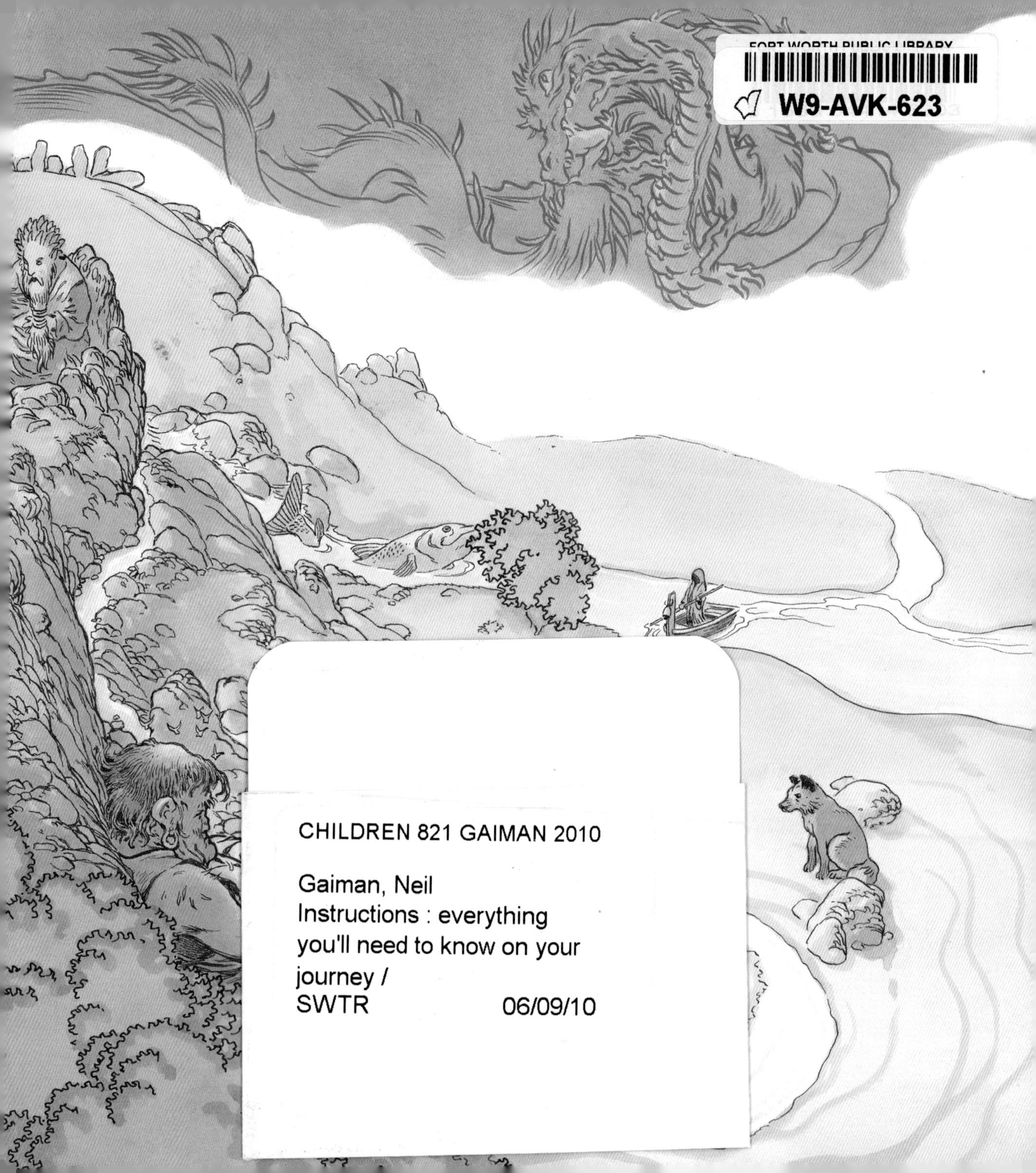

NEIL GAIMAN

INSTRUCTIONS

CHARLES VESS

*This one is for Terri Windling, for going on
ahead and illuminating the twisting path through the wild wood. —CV*

*For Ellen Kushner & Delia Sherman,
for coming back and telling us what they found. —NG*

HARPER
An Imprint of HarperCollinsPublishers

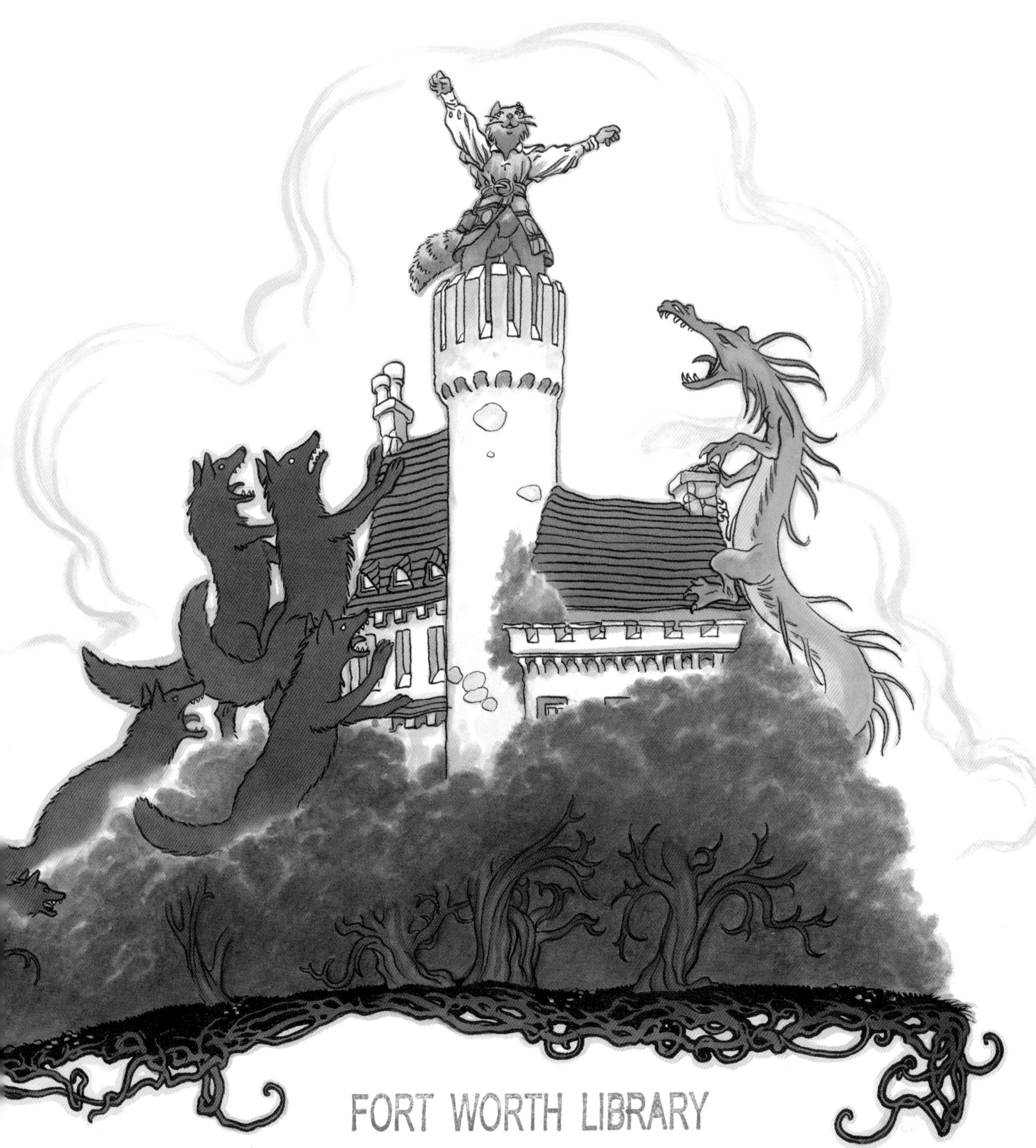

Touch the wooden gate in the wall you never
saw before,

Say "please" before you open the latch,
go through,

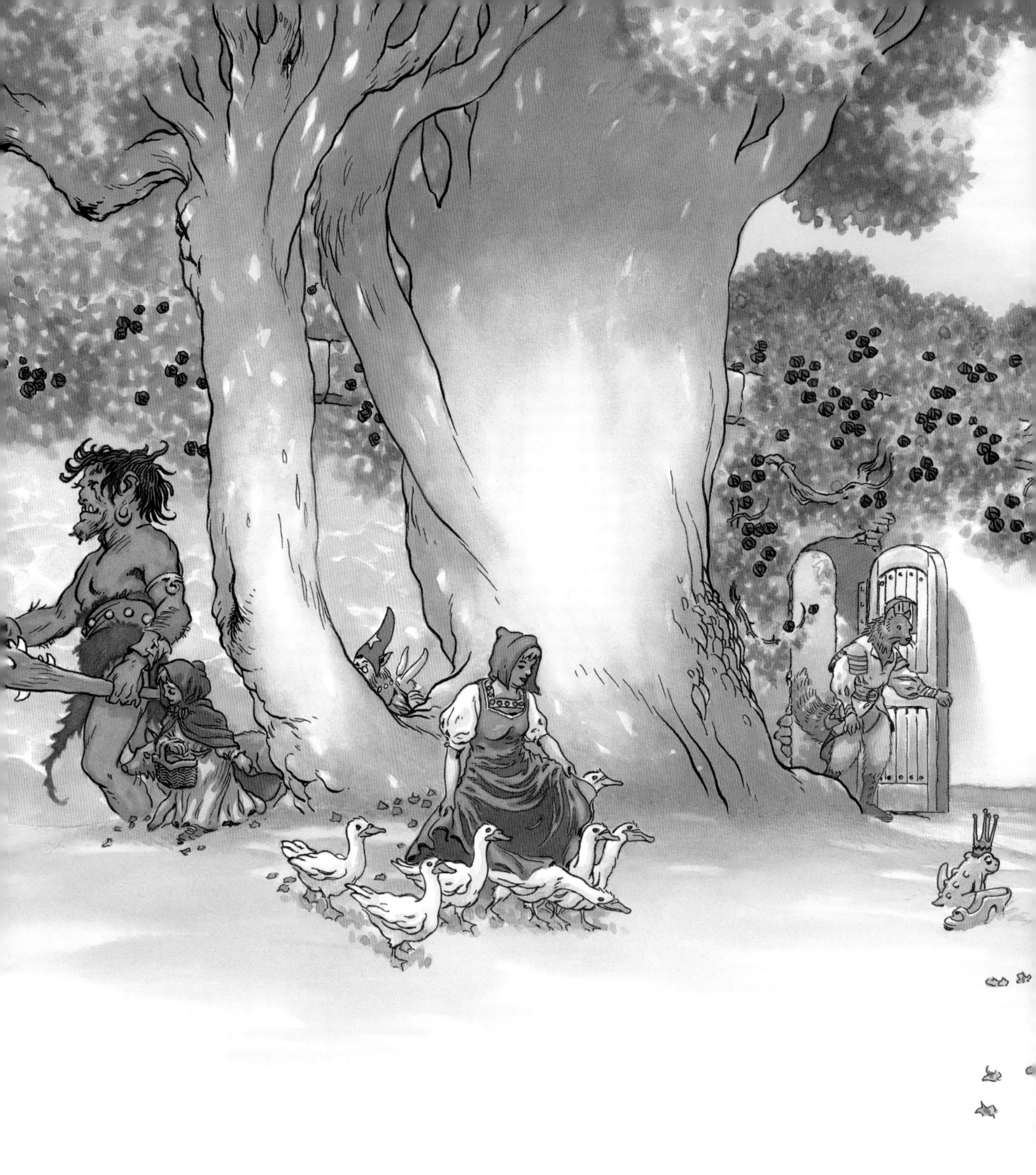

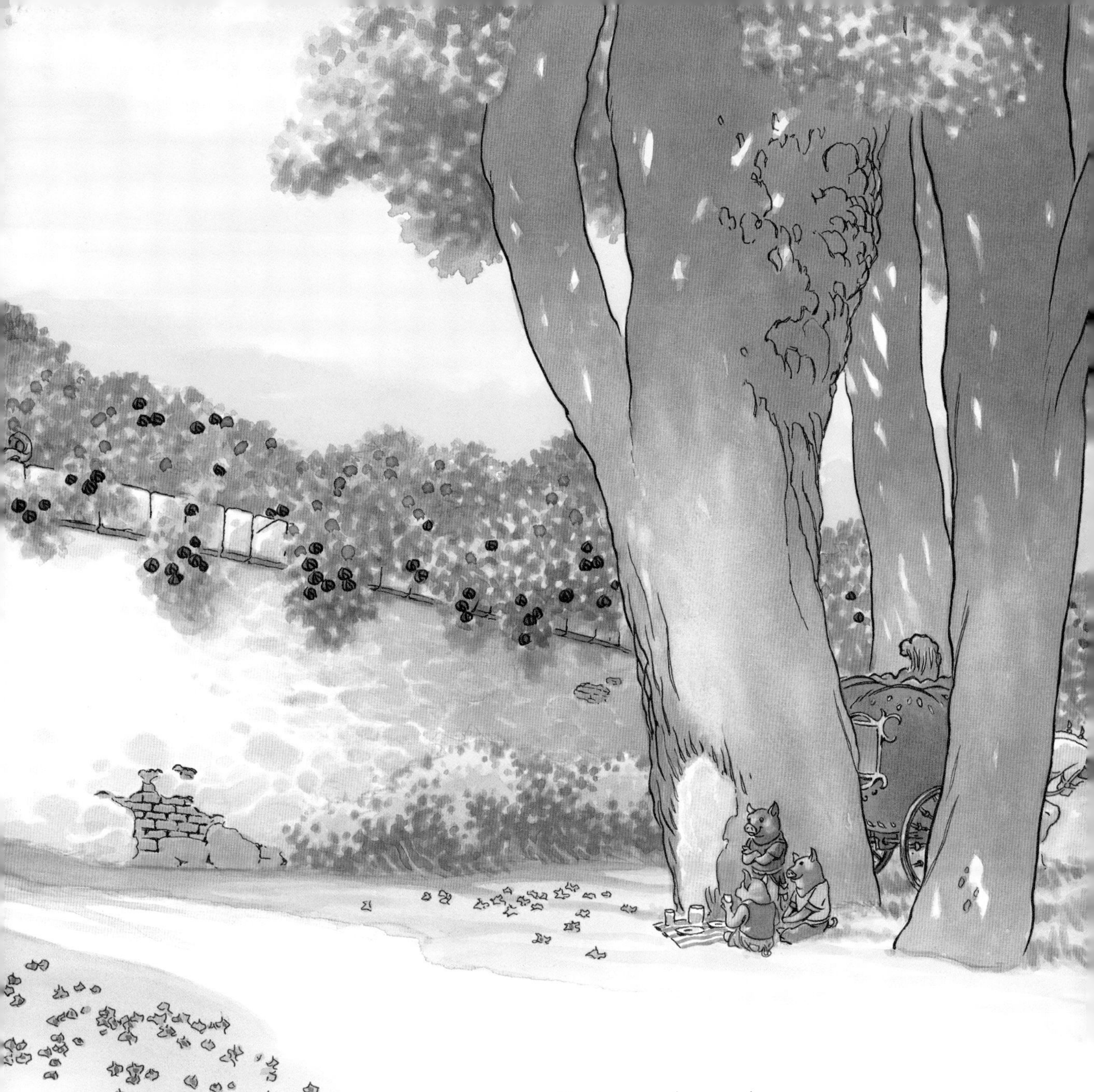

walk down the path.

A red metal imp hangs from the green-painted
front door,
as a knocker,

do not touch it; it will bite your fingers.

Walk through the house.
Take nothing.
Eat nothing.

However,
if any creature tells you that it hungers,
feed it.
If it tells you that it is dirty,
clean it.
If it cries to you that it hurts,
if you can,
ease its pain.

From the back garden you will be able to see the
wild wood.

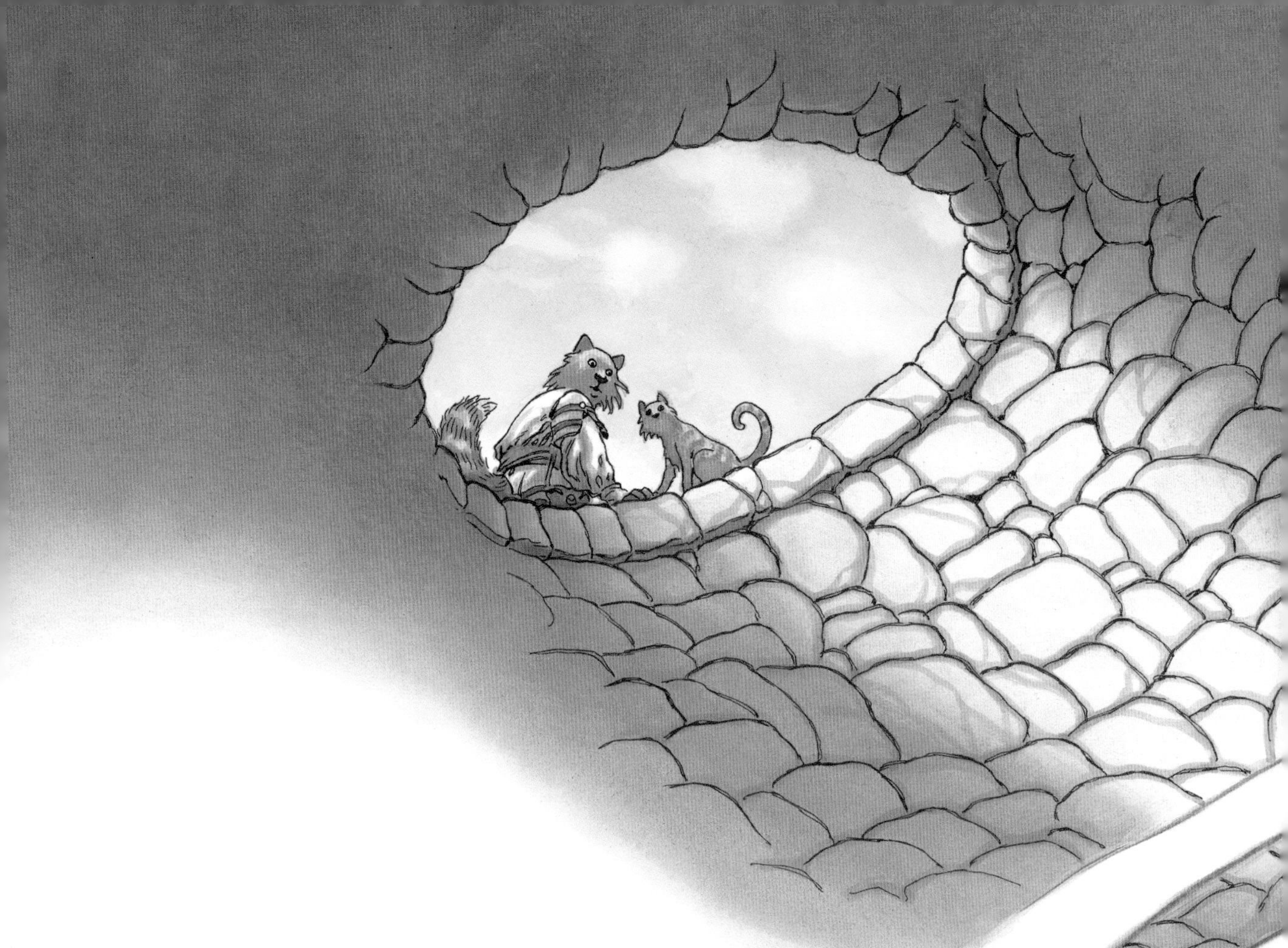

The deep well you walk past leads to Winter's
realm;
there is another land at the bottom of it.
If you turn around here,
you can walk back, safely;
you will lose no face.

I will think no less of you.

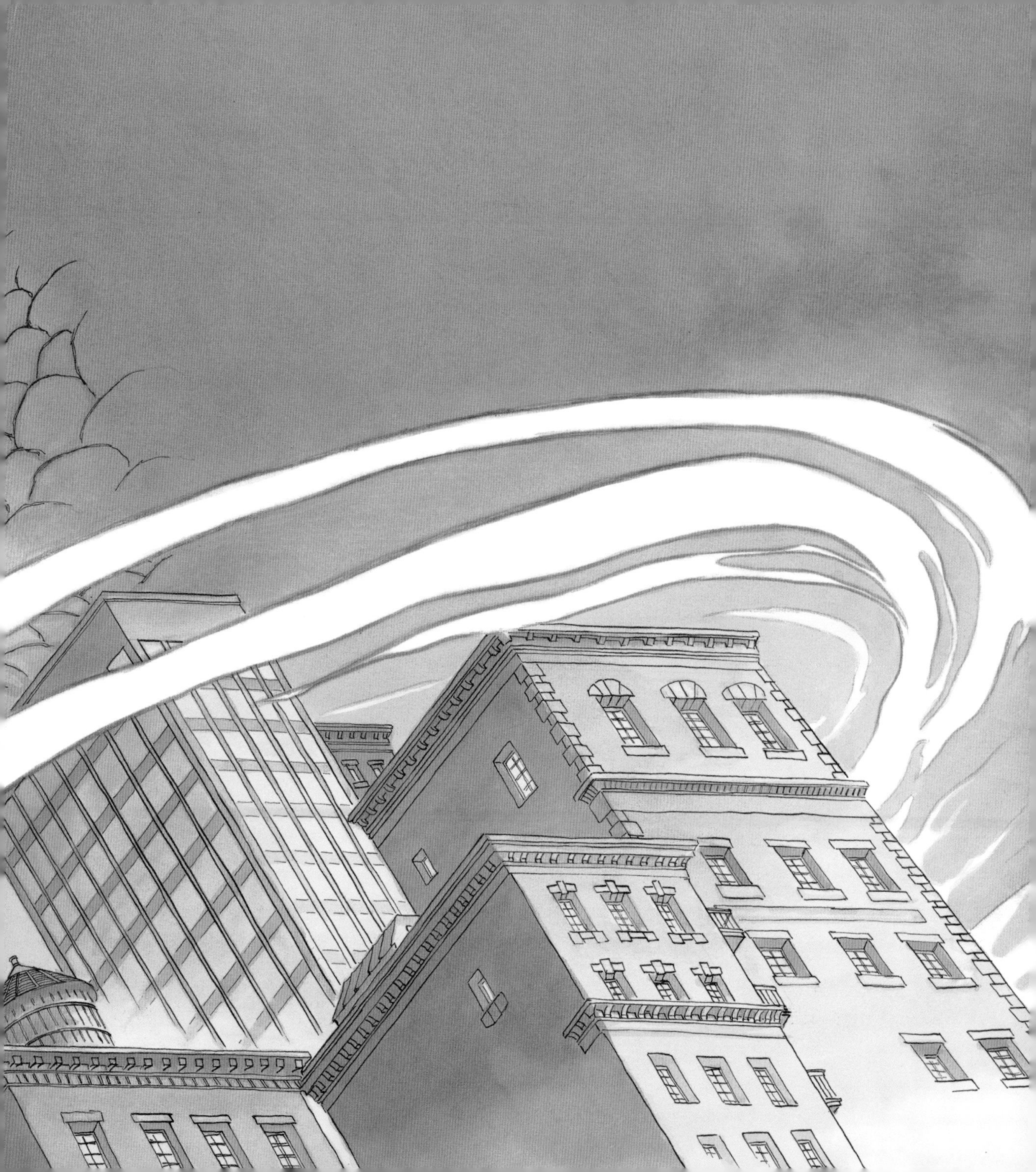

Once through the
garden you will
be in the wood.
The trees are old. Eyes peer
from the undergrowth.

Beneath a twisted oak
sits an old woman.
She may ask for
something;
give it to her. She
will point the way to
the castle.

Inside it are
three princesses.

Do not trust
the youngest.

Walk on.

In the clearing beyond the castle the twelve months sit about a fire, warming their feet, exchanging tales.

They may do favors for you, if you are polite.

You may pick strawberries in December's frost.

Trust the wolves, but do not tell them where
you are going.

The river can be crossed by the ferry.
The ferryman will take you.

(The answer to his question is this:
If he hands the oar to his passenger,
he will be free to leave the boat.

Only tell him this from a safe distance.)

If an eagle
gives you a feather,
keep it safe.

Remember:
that giants sleep too soundly;
that witches are often betrayed by their appetites;

dragons have one soft spot,
somewhere, always;
hearts can be well-hidden,
and you betray them with your tongue.

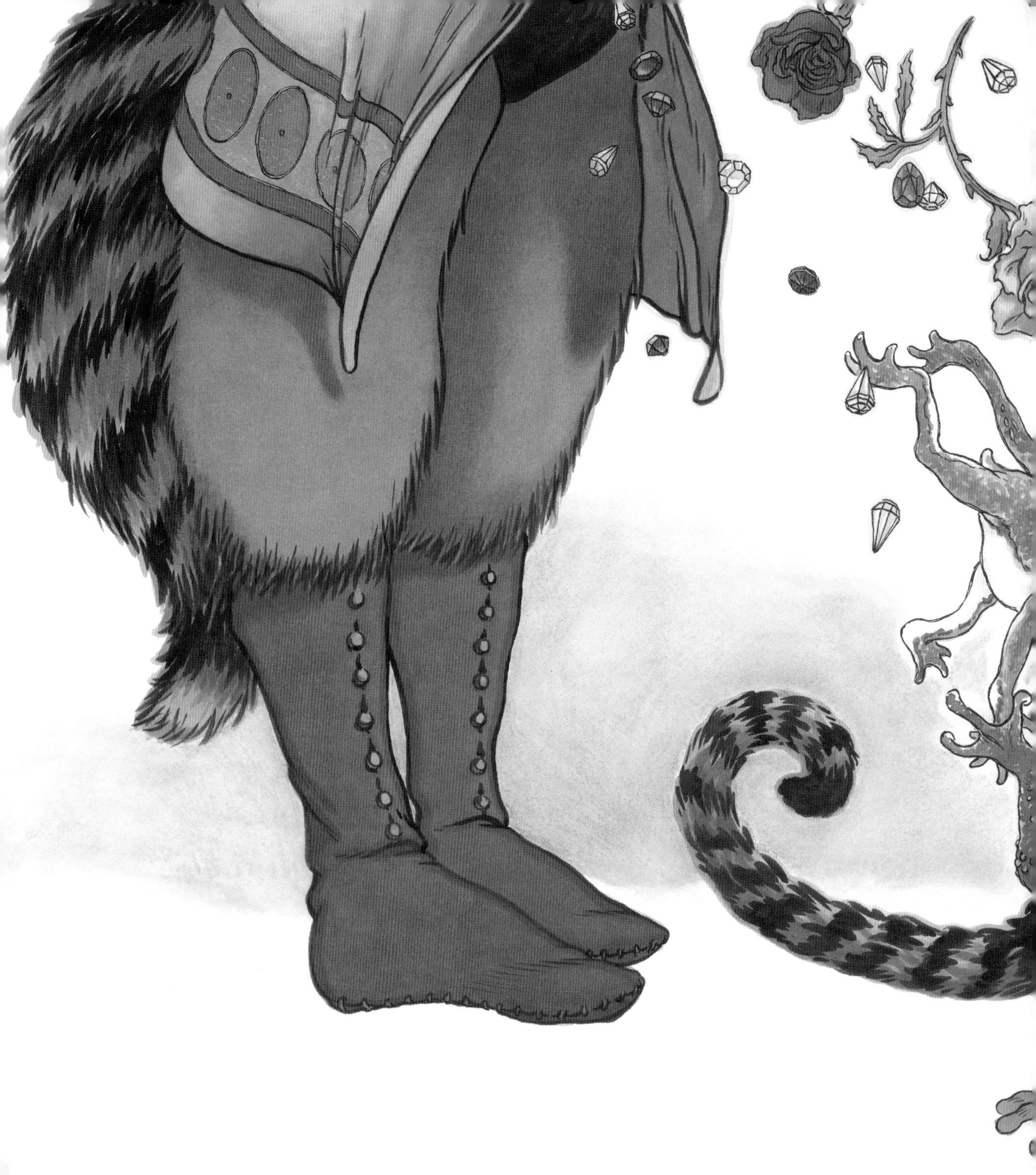

Do not be jealous of your sister:
know that diamonds and roses
are as uncomfortable when they tumble from
        one's lips as toads and frogs:
colder, too, and sharper, and they cut.

Remember your name.

Do not lose hope—
what you seek will
be found.

Trust ghosts.
Trust those that
you have helped to
help you in their turn.

Trust dreams.

Trust your heart,
and trust
your
story.

When you come back,
   return the way you came.
Favors will be returned,
   debts will be repaid.

Do not forget your manners.
Do not look back.

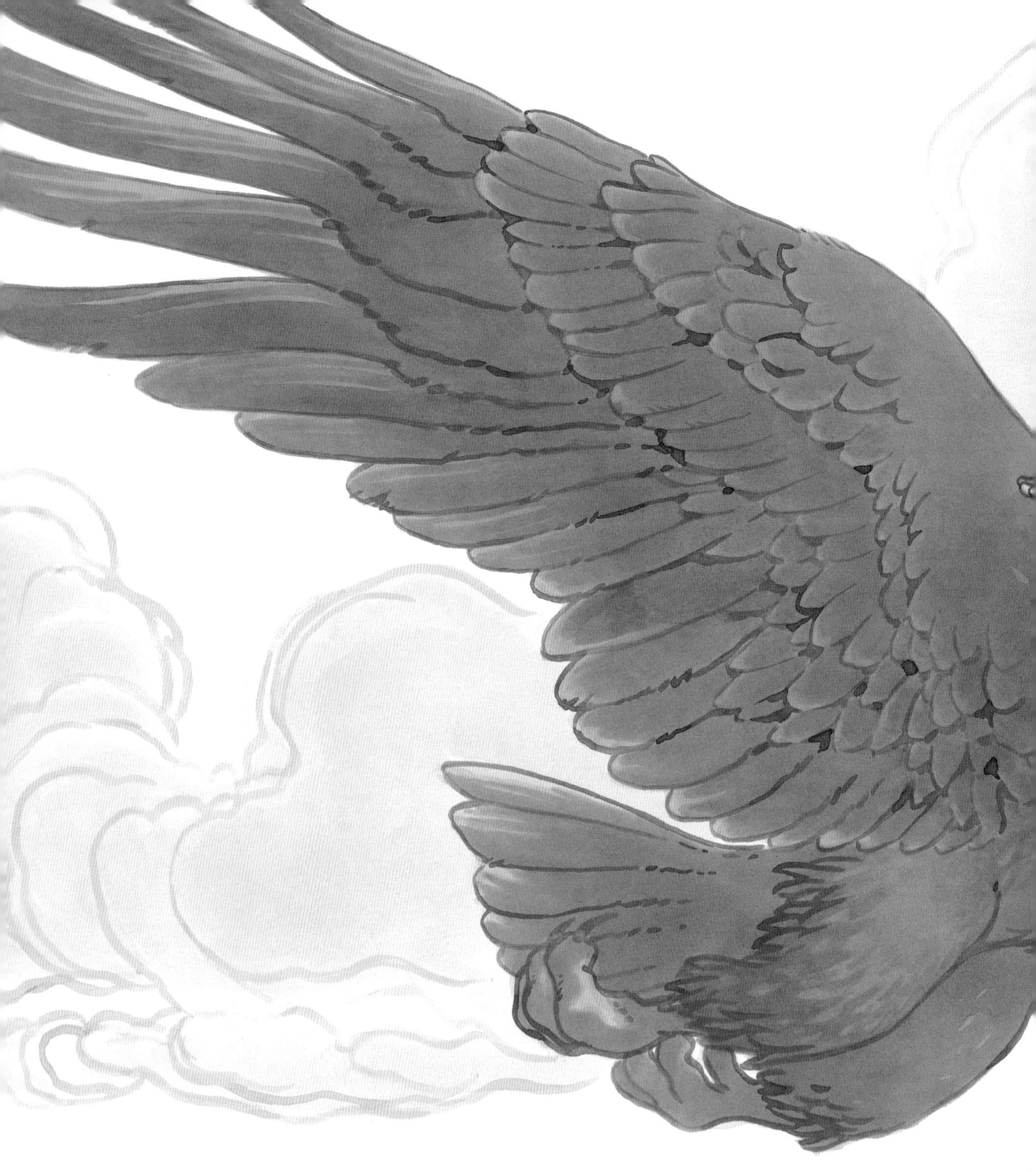

Ride the wise eagle
(you shall not fall).

Ride the silver fish
(you will not drown).

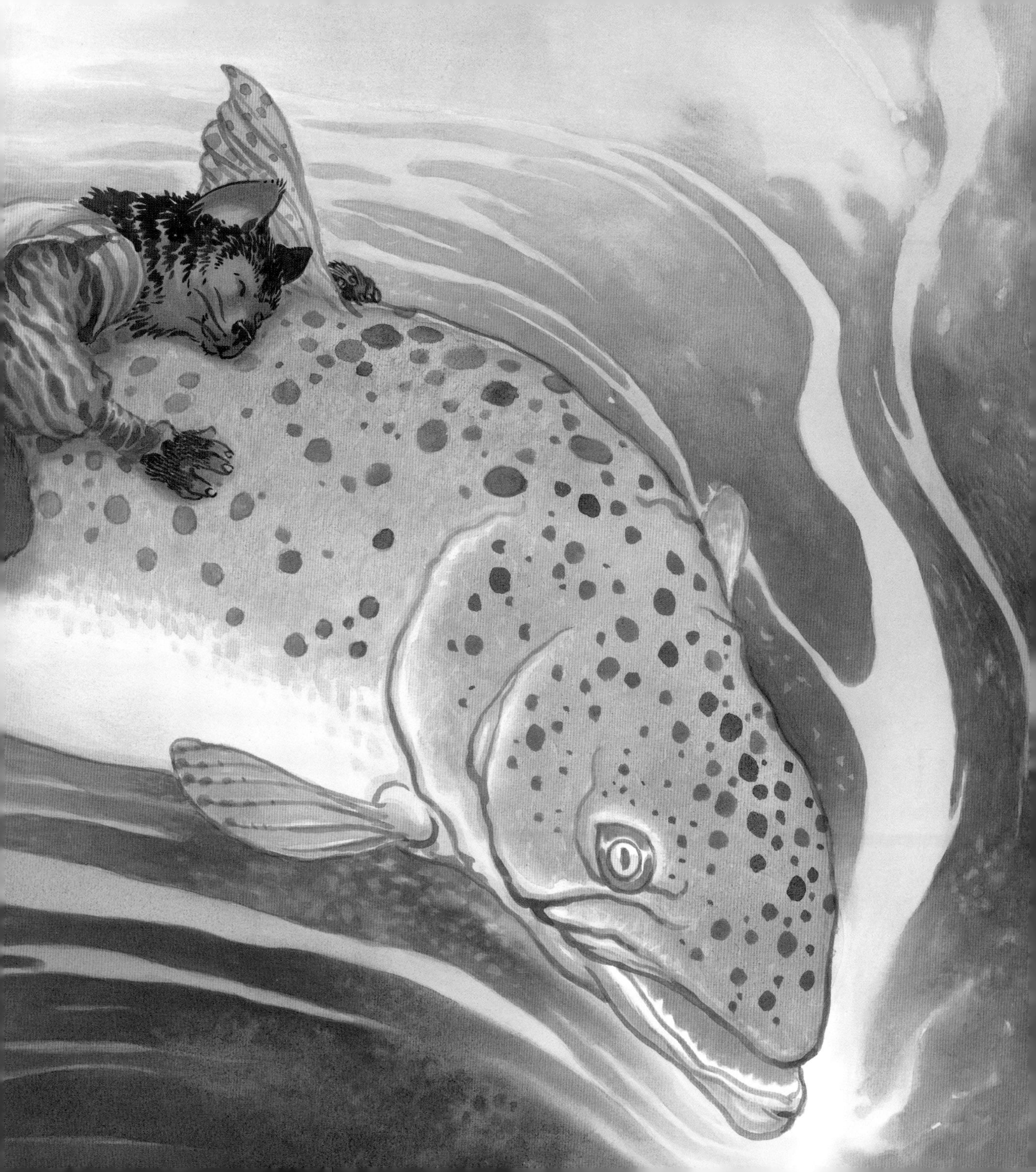

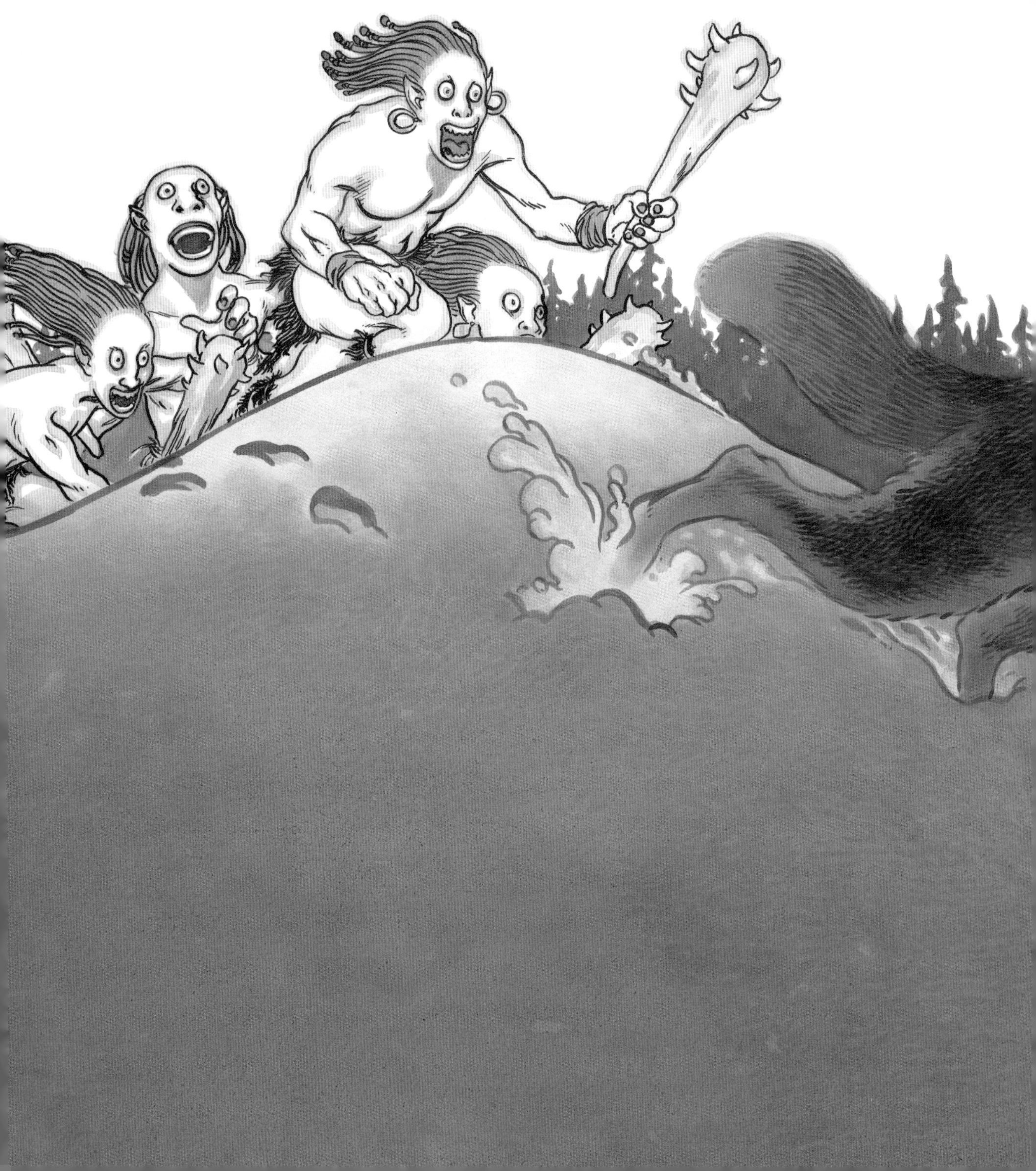

Ride the grey wolf
(hold tightly to his fur).

There is a worm at the heart of the tower;
that is why it will not stand.

When you reach the little house,
    the place your journey started,
you will recognize it, although it will seem
    much smaller than you remember.
Walk up the path, and through the garden
    gate you never saw before but once.

And then go home.

Or make a home.

Or rest.